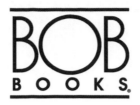

The
New Puppy

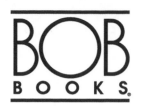

The New Puppy

by LYNN MASLEN KERTELL
illustrated by SUE HENDRA

SCHOLASTIC INC.

ISBN 978-1-338-80514-7

10 9 8 7 6 5 4 3 2 1   22 23 24 25 26

Printed in the U.S.A.   113
This edition first printing 2022

Jack and Anna want a puppy.

A puppy is a friend.

A puppy likes to play.

"A puppy is a lot of work," say Mom and Dad.

"Puppies need to be fed," says Dad.

"Puppies need to go out," says Mom.

"We will take care of it,"
the kids say.

Jack and Anna can do a good job.

There are many dogs at the pet shelter.

Big dogs, small dogs,
fluffy dogs, shaggy dogs.

Jack and Anna like
the brown puppy.

The puppy gives Anna a kiss.

"What will you name your pet?"
asks Mom.

"We can call him Buddy!"
says Jack.

Buddy loves to chase a ball.

He loves to tug a rope.

Jack and Anna want to draw.

Buddy wants to help.

Jack and Anna make a fort.

Buddy jumps in.

"Time to go out," says Mom.

Buddy runs and runs.

Anna gives Buddy his dinner.

Jack gives him water.

Buddy is tired.

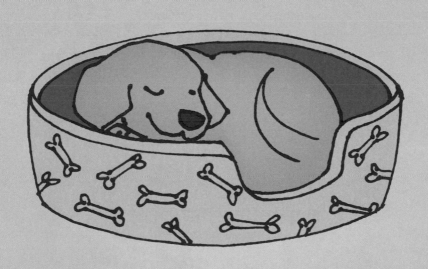

Buddy falls fast asleep.

Tomorrow, Buddy will be ready
to play again.

BOB BOOKS.

The Complete Bob Books® Series

READING READINESS   STAGE 1: STARTING TO READ

MY FIRST   MY FIRST   SET 1   MORE   FIRST   RHYMING
BOB BOOKS ®   BOB BOOKS ®   BEGINNING   BEGINNING   STORIES   WORDS
PRE-READING   ALPHABET   READERS   READERS
SKILLS

STAGE 2: EMERGING READER   STAGE 3: DEVELOPING READER

ADVANCING   SIGHT WORDS   ANIMAL   SIGHT WORDS   WORD   COMPLEX   LONG
BEGINNERS   KINDERGARTEN   STORIES   FIRST GRADE   FAMILIES   WORDS   VOWELS

SCHOLASTIC

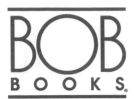